This Little Tiger book belongs to:

_____

_____

_____

*For Ian, love always*
~ E. B.

*For Levi – our smallest bun*
~ J. C.

LITTLE TIGER PRESS LTD,
an imprint of the Little Tiger Group
1 Coda Studios, 189 Munster Road, London SW6 6AW
www.littletiger.co.uk

First published in Great Britain 2007
This edition published 2020
Text copyright © Elizabeth Baguley 2007, 2020
Illustrations copyright © Jane Chapman 2007
Visit Jane Chapman at www.chapmanandwarnes.com
Elizabeth Baguley and Jane Chapman have asserted their rights to
be identified as the author and illustrator of this work under the Copyright,
Designs and Patents Act, 1988 • A CIP catalogue record for this book
is available from the British Library • All rights reserved

LTP/2700/3266/0620 • ISBN 978-1-78881-812-4
Manufactured, printed, and assembled in Foshan, China.
Second printing, June 2020
2 4 6 8 10 9 7 5 3

# A Long Way from Home

by Elizabeth Baguley          Illustrated by Jane Chapman

LiTTLE TiGER

LONDON

At bedtime in the burrow,
Moz was squished and squashed
by sleepy rabbits.
 "Oh no!" he tutted. "Crumplings!
Move over, Tam."

Tam squeezed over then folded her arms round Moz, using him as a hot water bottle.

"Too hot!" muttered Moz.
"Too many rabbits!"
So out into the night he went.

"What are you doing out here, Smallest Bun?"
asked Albatross, swooping down.

"There's no room," snuffled Moz. "And my
sister, Tam, is always squashing me."

"But she's your best friend!"

"It doesn't stop her squashing me," said Moz.

So, to cheer him up, Albatross told Moz
about the land of the North Star, where there
was sky space and snow space.

"No rabbits there!" sighed Moz. "I wish
I could come with you to the frozen North."

"Hop on, then, Smallest Bun," Albatross said.

Moz squeaked as Albatross lifted into the air.

Under the moon and over the wind she flew. As she soared high, high, higher, Moz held out his paws like wings.

"I'm flying!" he cried.

"Hold tight! It's the North Star!" Albatross shouted.

From the North Star
came a wild tornado
of snow, and before
Moz could take hold
of Albatross, he had
toppled into the storm.
Swept on the wind, he
tumbled and rolled . . .

down . . .

and down . . .

to land *puff!*
in a snowdrift.

Moz was all alone and for a moment he was afraid.
Then he looked around at the empty white space
and shook himself with excitement.
"No squish!" he cried. "No squash!"

Moz danced solo in the snow. He skated
and skimmed and threw snowballs, but
then *whoosh!* he was slipping down an
ice slide, going faster and faster.

Moz skidded to a stop. Oh no!
There were rabbits everywhere!
As he opened his mouth to protest,
the other rabbits did too—but the
only sound was Moz's tiny squeak.

"Mirror rabbits!" he gasped.
These weren't real rabbits,
just reflections in the ice.

Moz was in an ice cave, an ice hall, an ice palace!
It was as big as space and as quiet as silence.
And there was no one there but him.

In the mirror-walls Moz saw himself like
a king, his fluff grand with ice crystals.

Moz made a cool, roomy snow-nest.
"No nest-sharings!" he pronounced
and lay royally down to sleep.

When Moz woke, his fluff
was frozen and he was cold
to the bone. Shivering in his
lonely bed, he thought about
his snuggly sister Tam, squeezed
into the nest with all the sleepy
night-snufflings of his family.
Even his tears froze. How he
longed to go home!

So, out of the palace he crawled,
slipping and slithering up the ice slide
until he came out under the open
sky where the stony moon shone.
   "Albatross!" shouted Moz.
"Where are you?"
   There was no answer, only the
empty creaking of the ice.

But there! A feathery whisper on the wind. Moz looked up and saw wide wings. It was Albatross!

"Smallest Bun!" she said, relieved. "I've been looking for you everywhere!"

She swung Moz onto her back
and gratefully he nestled into
her warm down, thinking only
of home.

Back in the nest, Tam rolled over.
Moz was wonderfully squished and squashed;
he was gorgeously crumpled and crammed.
He was Tam's hot water bottle. He snuggled
into her fluff and, with a sigh, he fell to sleep.